Natalie Wittfang

HIDE AND SEEK
IN THE
YELLOW HOUSE

HIDE AND SEEK
in the
YELLOW HOUSE

by

AGATHA ROSE

illustrated by

KATE SPOHN

VIKING

VIKING
Published by the Penguin Group
Viking Penguin, a division of Penguin Books USA Inc.,
375 Hudson Street, New York, New York 10014, U.S.A.
Penguin Books Ltd, 27 Wrights Lane, London W8 5TZ, England
Penguin Books Australia Ltd, Ringwood, Victoria, Australia
Penguin Books Canada Ltd, 10 Alcorn Avenue, Toronto, Ontario, Canada M4V 3B2
Penguin Books (N.Z.) Ltd, 182–190 Wairau Road, Auckland 10, New Zealand

Penguin Books Ltd, Registered Offices: Harmondsworth, Middlesex, England

First published in 1992 by Viking Penguin, a division of Penguin Books USA Inc.

1   3   5   7   9   10   8   6   4   2

Text copyright © Agatha Rose, 1992
Illustrations copyright © Kate Spohn, 1992
All rights reserved

Library of Congress Cataloging-in-Publication Data
Rose, Agatha.
Hide-and-seek in the yellow house / by Agatha Rose ;
illustrated by Kate Spohn.   p.   cm.
Summary: A mischievous kitten leads his mother on a merry chase
of hide-and-seek throughout the tiny world that is their home.
ISBN 0-670-84383-0
[1. Cats — Fiction. 2. Hide-and-seek — Fiction.] I. Spohn, Kate, ill.   II. Title.
PZ7.R7143Hi   1992   [E] — dc20   91-29848   CIP   AC

Printed in Singapore
Set in Frutiger 57 Condensed

To Corey

In the yellow house,

Mother Cat is searching
for her kitten,

and she calls him:
"Mack! Mack! Mack!"

She sees him sitting
in the window.

Now he isn't there.
"Mack! Mack! Mack!"

She sees him playing
in the bushes.

Now he isn't there.
"Mack! Mack! Mack!"

She sees him eating
from their food dish.

Now he isn't there.

She sees him standing
on the table.

Now he isn't there.
"Mack! Mack! Mack!"

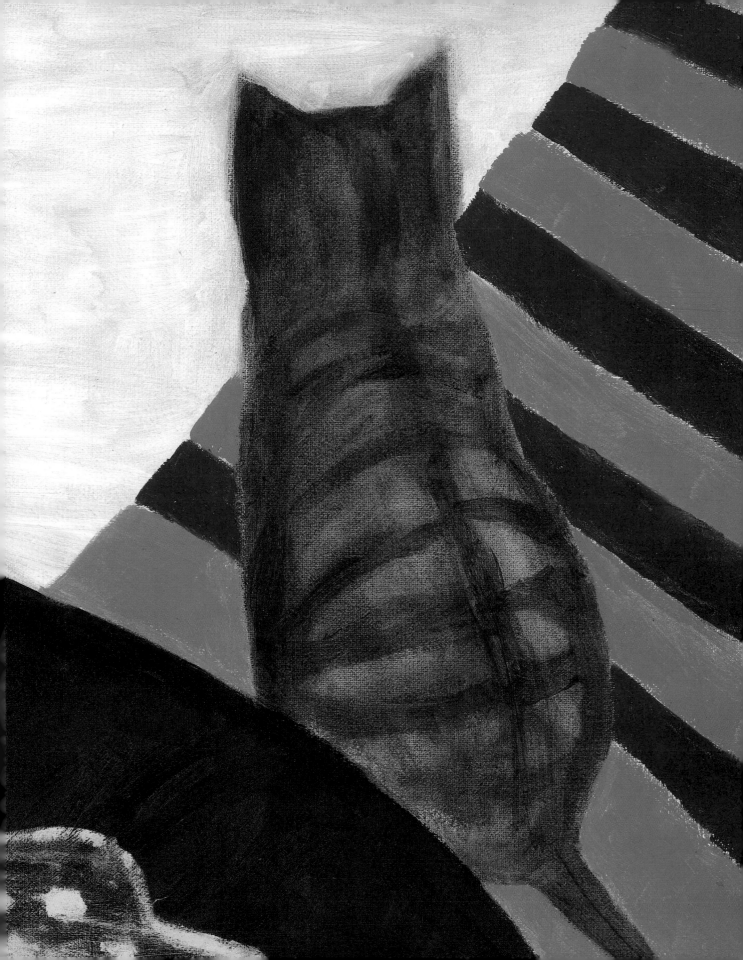

She complains:
"Where can my
little kitten be?"
"Mew! Mew!"

"Oh, here you are,
right beside me!"

And Mother Cat starts to wash
her kitten, Mack.